Chasing Unicorns

SWANWICK WRITERS

Copyright © 2017 Individual Contributors

Maggie Kay (*Celebrating Sisterhood*)

Elizabeth Hopkinson (*Chasing Unicorns*)

Fay Wentworth (*Whisper in the Wind*)

Brian Lockett (*Sir Humphrey Appleby Meets William Shakespeare*)

Elizabeth Ducie (*The Pop Star and the Businessman*)

Val Williamson (*At the Eleventh Hour*)

Julia Pattison (*Zoe's Birthday Treat*)

Pat Belford (*A Surprise in the Jungle*)

Helen Ellwood (*Spreading Magic*)

Julia Pattison (*Bramwell and the Spider*)

Katy Clarke (*A Sign of Peace*)

Karen Rogerson (*Cover illustration*)

All rights reserved. No part of this publication may be reproduced, stored in or introduced into a retrieval system, or transmitted in any form or by any means (electronic, mechanical, photocopying, recording or otherwise), without the prior written permission of the copyright owner.

Edited by Elizabeth Ducie, Diana Wimbs and Andrew Marsh

Published in 2017 by Chudleigh Phoenix Publications

Printed by Create Space

ISBN-10: 1977891179
ISBN-13: 978-1977891174

DEDICATION

To our friend, Katy Clarke; taken from us far too soon, but never forgotten

CONTENTS

FOREWORD i

CELEBRATING SISTERHOOD 1

CHASING UNICORNS 5

WHISPER IN THE WIND 9

SIR HUMPHREY APPLEBY MEETS WILLIAM SHAKESPEARE 13

THE POP STAR AND THE BUSINESS MAN 20

AT THE ELEVENTH HOUR 25

ZOE'S BIRTHDAY TREAT 31

A SURPRISE IN THE JUNGLE 33

SPREADING MAGIC 35

BRAMWELL AND THE SPIDER 39

A SIGN OF PEACE 41

ABOUT THE AUTHORS 44

THE MAGIC OF SWANWICK 46

FOREWORD

Katy Clarke was a brave, funny and inspiring lady who loved family and friends, words and writing, Scotland, history, music and spirituality. A lot of her own writing was historical human interest, like the piece about her great grandfather reproduced at the end of this book. As well as being a wonderful mum, writer and writing tutor, wherever Katy went she made friends and changed people's lives for the better. Latterly, she was a founder member of discussion group Conscious Evolution and Ipplepen local history group in Devon. When living in Dorset, she led the campaign to save Highcliffe Castle. In Ayr, Scotland, where Katy brought up her family, she was an active member of the Robert Burns Society and became the first ever woman President. She also supported and advocated for health and well-being organisations throughout her life.

After Katy died, I signed up for a charity walk in aid of Rowcroft Hospice and collected some very generous sponsorship from Katy's friends and family. But then the walk was cancelled! I wanted to do something in Katy's memory and in acknowledgement of both the sponsorship and the wonderful support that this part of Devon receives from the staff at Rowcroft. Chatting with my husband in the taxi from the airport to our holiday villa in Portugal, the idea *Chasing Unicorns* was born.

It was Katy who introduced me to the Writers' Summer School and therefore it seemed obvious to involve other Swanwickers in the project, both as writers and editors. The brief was for stories and other pieces of writing that reflect some of the things that meant so much to Katy.

Katy's daughter, Karen, designed the cover. Katy's sister, Maggie Kay, wrote the moving opening letter and also provided the wonderful article from Katy herself that closes the book.

Thank you for buying this book and supporting the cause.

Elizabeth Ducie
October 2017

CELEBRATING SISTERHOOD

Maggie Kay (Srimati)

Dearest Sis

At my birthday parties, you always tell the tale of how, as an eight year old girl, Mum tied a ribbon in your hair one morning between contractions. Later, newborn sister arrived, you walked to the local shop and bought me a soother in the shape of a teddy bear with your own pocket money.

And of how, a few months after that, on summer holiday, the baby sitter said "You may hold your sister if she wakes." So you pinched me. And I woke. And cried. And you felt terrible about it. The baby sitter didn't understand why you were crying too as you held me.

Back home we shared a bedroom in the attic. Twin beds in 'non-identical twin' halves. Mine, so neat—teddies in a row. Yours, alive with teenage shape and colour—make up, guitar, clothes. "Angie Baby" and Barry White woke us on cold winter mornings, recorded from radio onto cassette. You loved the music charts and always remembered who sang what and when—forever our pop music expert.

The eight years between us placed us a world apart. Yet when I was eight and you 16, I fell for your first love, Frank, too, snuggling up to him on the sitting room sofa whilst he sang me "Pretty Little Girl in a Blue Dress."

Frank was guest of honour at my birthday party (the one where I broke into tears because I wasn't winning 'move the pea'—too much emotion on my special day), wearing my best blue dress, of course.

And when I was 16, I also fell for an attractive, dark haired boy with a motorbike, who looked uncannily like your Frank. Motorbike parked in the same spot Frank's once occupied, John was my first love.

You seemed so grown up—working, writing poems, getting serious with a handsome air traffic controller, Pete. Even more so, when, late one Christmas eve, you woke me excitedly as I was going off to sleep, "Pete has proposed!" you told me breathlessly. I wore my first adult underwear with that bridesmaid's dress, thrilled to be growing up too.

Happily expanding into our attic bedroom all by myself, I rearranged one bed under the alcove to break the symmetry and painted the woodwork chocolate brown. I loved having my own space.

But I missed you. And wrote my first ever published article in *Jackie Magazine* titled TLSAOBSF: The Little Sisters' Appreciation of Big Sisters Federation, explaining how my new found space came with a loss. I was realising how much you'd been there for me, looking out for me, giving advice.

Throughout the coming years, you 'got me' like no other—understanding and supporting me with such care and wisdom. When we came to stay, you treated my teenage boyfriend, John, and me as adults. It was amazing to feel so respected and trusted.

I observed you making a wonderful job of creating a home and family. After a difficult start bringing a baby to term, you became a mother. Holding your first born, Karen, in my arms, an explosion of love like I'd never known before washed through me. A tiny taste of my own motherhood to come.

Sleeping in the alcove bed, staying the night to visit Dad in hospital, you were there the morning Mum called upstairs, "Your dad's condition is deteriorating." We saw Dad's newly vacated body together and felt his spirit liberated. And you were still staying a few nights later, when he came to 'visit' from the other side.

I admired you relishing your beautiful home and family whilst I went off in quite a different direction. And you always honoured my choices, too, the first to gladly call me 'Srimati' when I was ordained as a Buddhist, understanding the significance of the spiritual path I was following.

My visits to you in lovely Ayrshire were havens of love, beauty, welcome and family—listening to Clannad in the car as we sped along the coast road to Culzean Castle, staying up until 3am talking passionately about life beyond death, sharing our lives and our stories. And Love. And Truth.

When my son Jamie burst into our world unexpectedly, you said you always knew I'd have my own child. And when I navigated the painful days of separating the family a few years later, you were the first I turned to. Totally non-judgemental, any problem is always safe with you.

During those first six months in Devon I must have spoken to you every day on my new-fangled mobile phone from my temporary caravan. My heart breaking with a million griefs, disoriented and alone, you SO got me through that time, dear sister.

Until I met the most amazing man (having moved to the cottage you had foreseen with your inner eye). The week Pat and I truly connected, you were with Gran, sharing her passage to the other side with me daily by phone. You let me hear Gran breathing and told me how utterly beautiful and peaceful she looked when she finally died. I felt like I was there too.

Gran transitioned the night Pat and I truly connected and said "I see you" to one another. And six weeks later, without hesitation, you offered him some of her ashes to scatter—on a highland glen overlooking Loch Lomond—welcoming him into our clan. You 'saw' him too.

The next year, you helped create our wonderful riverside wedding. Styling my hair and make up, preparing the ritual space, telling stories, singing songs ("God help the Mister that comes between me and my sister") and reading out a poem you wrote for the occasion, you were the star of the wedding video!

Soon, you followed me to Devon, yourself seeking refuge amidst tumultuous changes. You made great friends with my closest friend Susanne and quickly with many more. A few months after you moved, a high street shop vendor said to me (when she heard my Scottish accent) "Oh you must be KATY'S sister!" as though I was the newcomer to town.

You found you were at home in the Totnes and Newton Abbot cafe scene and we enjoyed many a catch up over coffee. Likewise in charity shops where you exercised your exceptional eye for good looking outfits. It wasn't long before my 'Katy Collection' wardrobe outnumbered my own clothes!

After a few false starts, you met such a special, special man. I never heard you chuckle like that before. Such deep contentment for the first time. Yet it was to be cruelly plucked away. How amazing that the night before Mike's sudden passing, we three had talked long and deeply of love and God and life after death.

The next morning, I was there with you while the ambulance crew did their best to revive Mike. You came back home with Pat and me that night, wracked with shock and grief, sleepless by the open fire. And you were never quite the same happy Katy again.

Nonetheless, you didn't give up. Inch by inch, you slowly recovered and rebuilt, your soul matured beyond measure. And settled in your beautiful Thimble Cottage and made your mark in the immediate and wider community and found love again. Wow!

No matter what is going on for you, you always care, you always have so much to give. And it is always you I turn to. You were there for me during those rocky months when Pat's health broke down. And it is you I imagine fleeing to if he and I ever have an argument!

I couldn't be there enough for you, though. Overwhelmed by the demands of Pat's poor health, bringing up Jamie, running a business, maintaining a house, making a living, I rarely had time to offer. (You were not the only one—as every friend of mine will tell you!)

The pain of that was real for us both, but we never quarrelled and only twice had a day or two of tension. And finally (brought to the fore by current challenges), it was completely resolved in recent months. I let go of my defensive armour. And cried. And said sorry. And you understood. And there was nothing to forgive.

Almost exactly a year ago, on my birthday, we met at the Seven Stars Hotel in Totnes. You were full of fun and had arranged a secret birthday cake and candle to be brought out to me. I loved it! More importantly, we were together again having been kept somewhat apart in recent months by a so called 'best friend' (who you foresaw was not as she seemed.) You were glad I had now seen through that.

It's nearly my birthday again. What a journey this year has been, a journey you have met with such awesome courage and grace. Who would have guessed what lay ahead as I blew out that birthday candle last year?

My darling sister, you are leading the way again. (I'm remembering your fortune cookie in the summer which said you would be a leader.) This time, the rite of passage you are leading is not first love or getting married or becoming a mother. This time, you are leading the way into the Beyond.

Though it utterly breaks my heart, I also know this passage will yield gifts. I will learn something about my own inevitable passing. And as my heart breaks further open, I will bond closer and closer to loved ones (that's happening already). And I know you and I will always, ALWAYS be in communion - beyond life, death, time and space.

My spirit guide, Clarion, tells me "There is nothing to do. Carry on meeting each day with integrity and all shall be well." That is very much how you are meeting this, my precious sis. I am in awe of that. I thank God for you and all we have shared, now and forever more.

Love is all.

Maggie Kay.

[*I wrote this before my birthday in early February 2017, just as we were learning not much more could be done to heal my darling sister. She passed away on 23rd April, our beloved late Gran's birthday, seeming like she'd waited to that special date on purpose. I never did share this letter with Katy as it didn't seem right at the time, so it is lovely to do so now as part of such a meaningful project.*]

CHASING UNICORNS

Elizabeth Hopkinson

"It begins with a gap between things. A scarce-felt tearing in the fabric of the cosmos. To the layman, this might seem like little more than a change in the light or a feeling of déjà vu. But once one becomes accustomed to such events, one learns to detect them, almost by instinct, and even to predict them, as one might predict an oncoming storm. For the paranaturalist, there is no greater pleasure than being present at these moments. The seam of reality slowly unpicks itself. You feel a tremor in the electro-magnetic field. And then, they come..."

I close Hedley's notebook, swallowing the lump in my throat. Five years on, and I can still hear his voice in those words. Purring like a great cat beside me in our two-man tent. Flank to flank, the warmth of him. Both of us watching through the circles of our binoculars. Observing, recording, measuring, counting.

"Nothing like the thrill of the chase, Lambie," he'd always say. And smile in that crooked way that made two wrinkles appear at the side of his mouth.

The tent feels enormous without him.

I pitched it where we always said we would. By the lake, half hidden under the trees. Sunset was beautiful, but I can already feel the slight tug of autumn on the late days of summer. Clear skies. Perfect conditions. The moorhens are fussing as they settle down among the reeds. A rabbit bumps around the back of the tent, bumps away again.

I'm waiting for them to come back.

"The Swanwick unicorn migration was first recorded by the monks of Beauchief Abbey

in 1349. *A surviving manuscript describes: a grete herd of unicornes in the starres upon St Lawrence Day. It also features in the diaries of Selina Wright of Butterley, whose entry for 12th August 1849 speaks of: the night of the Perseid meteors. The heavens opened, and unicorns galloped forth, so their hooves seemed to touch the very earth. I was never in my life so transported.*"

Unicorns were Hedley's passion long before that ghastly dinner dance threw us together. I remember summers at my aunt's, sitting on the veranda, hours after the others had gone to bed. His tales of student nights on the rooftops of St Andrew's, where a single unicorn came to graze in the quadrangle by moonlight. Childhood days spent roaming the moors, listening for the thunder of hooves.

"Come with me, Lambie. Agnes." His eyes grew soft. One thumb stroked the back of my hand. "What a team we'll make! We two."

We did everything together from the start. Pitching camp soon fell into a natural rhythm. Square lashing, collecting firewood, digging a latrine. Hedley could always pick the best terrain. I became expert at bribing guides.

The world has changed since the War. So many new countries, new borders, new governments. Boundaries dividing brother from brother. But in those first years, the Empire was open to us. We went everywhere: Rhodesia, Egypt, Malaya, Bengal. Our book was to be called: *Unicorns of the World and their Habitats*. The most comprehensive study of unicorns undertaken in modern times. Together, we had observed the Alpine unicorn with its goat like features, the lithe Oriental Kirin, the Hispanic unicorn with wings on its feet, and the stocky but swift Steppes variety. Our field journals became full to bursting with sketches, photographs, data, maps.

"What did I tell you?" Hedley would squeeze my shoulder in that boyish way of his. "Wait until the Natural History Museum see all this. There could be a Nobel Prize in it!" He would wink, with that crinkle-mouthed smile. "Couldn't do it without you, Lambie."

Lambie. No one had called me that but Hedley. A play on my Christian name. Agnes. The pure. The innocent.

"Unicorns can't resist a pure damsel. You do know that's why I married you?"

I would hit him on the head with the billy can. Gently, of course. We both knew the unicorn-and-maiden thing was an old wives' tale, but the joke never seemed to get old. He relied on me. Always had. We were a team, striving equally towards the same goal.

I don't know if I can do this without him.

He was called up in November 1939. They sent for me three months later. Top secret. Mother kept insisting to the last that they'd made a mistake, that married women didn't get called up. I couldn't tell her what I was doing. Punching holes and splicing tapes most of the time. And listening. Watching, observing, looking for patterns. They needed girls with languages and a good brain. The others were single, giggling and gossiping in the lodging house at night, fantasising about GIs. I missed the wide open spaces, warm nights sleeping under the stars. I missed Hedley.

We met in London, one time on leave. Walking around Green Park arm-in-arm, trying to pretend it was the Black Forest or the Amazon. Hedley looked tired; there were black smudges under his eyes. He couldn't speak of his work either, so we didn't try. A squirrel skittered past. The earth smelled of spring, as though it didn't know there was a war on. Hedley squeezed my arm.

"When all this is over, we'll do the Swanwick migration."

We'd talked of this numerous times, those nights in the Wadi and the Chittagong Hills. Hedley believed the unicorns returned once a century, at the time of the Perseid meteor shower. If he was correct, the next migration would be in 1949. Prove this, and he would have a status among paranaturalists akin to that of Sir Edmund Halley, with his comet.

I sighed, and pulled closer to him.

"What if it's still not over in '49?"

Hedley kissed me.

"It will be, Lambie. Keep your pecker up, old girl."

The sky darkens from pink to purple to black. A frog croaks, splashes. I can see the Evening Star. The Plough. Cassiopeia. I wriggle my blanket higher up my shoulder, unscrew my thermos. Patience. The life of a paranaturalist is one of constant waiting.

Other girls fretted about their sweethearts. Sent off to France, to Norway, to Burma, to the Sudan. Places whose wilder regions I could have described in detail. Dreading the fatal telegram: *Missing in Action.* And Hedley was shut up in a basement in London. Listening, waiting, observing, recording. I never even thought to worry. A man cannot die of tedium. Then one day in '44, he went to the shop for some cough sweets. Never made it to the shelter. Of all the telegrams I decoded, that was the one I couldn't make sense of. One of the girls came and took it out of my hand, eventually. They said I'd been staring for two hours.

I finish the last of the sweet tea, tip the dregs onto the grass. They never found a body. For months, I expected him to walk through the door, in thick, woollen knee socks and a khaki shirt. Binoculars around his neck and a pencil behind his ear. *Come on, Lambie. We need to set off, if we mean to catch the migration.* Mother wanted me to come back home after the War. I couldn't. Not chintz curtains, the smell of beeswax and mutton. I stayed on with the same landlady for a while. The War Office sent me Hedley's old equipment and notebooks. I'd read and re-read them, deep into the night, by the light of a paraffin lamp.

I knew I'd end up here. In Swanwick, on 12th August, 1949. Waiting for the meteor shower.

"A herd of migrating unicorns is one of the most magnificent sights in the paranatural kingdom. No description can do justice to the spectacle of flowing manes, galloping hooves, thrusting horns. One is witness to antiquity, a sight that was seen before cities, before humanity itself. One is looking back onto an age of gods and giants. A time of myth and magic, now long gone, but which - who knows? - may one day return."

The sky is inky black now. The stars are crystalline, littered across the heavens like diamond dust. A chill wind shakes the branches, but my blood begins to warm. A pulse throbs in my ears. There! It is beginning! A single shooting star draws a silver line across the sky. Then another. Then another. I wriggle out of the tent, my binoculars to my eyes. The heavens are alight with silver trails. Beneath my hips, there is a thrumming in the earth. A taste of magic on my tongue. The meteor trails grow longer, coalescing into a starry road. The light draws nearer, grows broader, more alive. From beyond the fields we know, comes the sound of a horse's whinny.

They are here. Thundering down the path of light, crossing the lake without making a ripple. Unicorns. Hundreds of them. A sea of backs and manes and thrusting horns. White, every one, but so much more than white. Opalescent. Luminous. Shimmering silver glass. Their horns refracting the rainbow like mother-of-pearl. On and on they gallop, across the lawn, past the sleeping house. The largest unicorn migration anywhere in the world. I come out of my tent and stand, my shadow a salute to their retreating backs.

And still they come. On and on, tossing their manes in the starlight, galloping to who-knows-where?

[I was honoured to be asked to write the title story for this anthology in memory of Katy, who I remember best for her Vice-chair announcements and Five Rhythms classes at Swanwick. (Woe betide anyone who turned up late!) I knew I wanted it to be a Swanwick story when I noticed unicorns in the furniture and stained glass windows of The Hayes. And with the 70th anniversary of the Writer's Summer School coming up, I knew that I wanted to set it in 1949, when the school first convened at The Hayes. The Perseid meteor showers are always a magical part of the Swanwick week, so it seemed only right that they should herald a migration of unicorns. I think Katy would like that.]

WHISPER IN THE WIND

Fay Wentworth

Marissa ran down the bank, gorse fronds catching her feet. Tall firs blocked the sunlight as she arrived, breathless, in the dell. Soft grasses swayed in the breeze and, as the firs fell away, the sunbeams caught her bare arms, arms enfolding daffodils; wild daffodils that she had picked from the spinney on the edge of the wood before the firs began and blighted the undergrowth. The frail yellow petals bobbed and bent and sap trickled from the broken stems, staining her skirt.

She drew a deep breath, stilling her gasps and then walked sedately through the door of the chapel, tucked into the corner of the dell, its old stones mellow in the sunshine. It was cool inside, stone floored, wooden pews rotting where the rain had pierced a broken window and left damp patches. Leaves scuttled into corners as the wind followed her footsteps and scurried through dust and debris.

Marissa walked quietly up the aisle, her eyes fixed on the heavy wooden cross, leaning slightly, on the unkempt altar. She leant forward and, very gently, opened her arms and allowed the daffodils to fall, higgledy-piggledy, against the cross; flower heads locked and entwined, stems criss-crossed. The cascade of green and yellow was suddenly caught by a beam of golden light as the sun escaped a cloud and hurried to pierce the grimy window to silhouette the young girl at the cross.

She turned and raised her eyes to the gentle warmth and then, overwhelmed, fell to her knees, her head resting against the damp stems that were tumbling over the altar.

She felt a touch on her arm and raised tearful eyes.

"Come, little one."

Her eyes filled with fear. He stepped back, a gentle smile softening the intensity of his gaze, a gaze that swept over her as cool as the sun-kissed sea and his hair seemed to sparkle in the sunshine, soft waves the colour of ripe corn. And she found her fear dissipating.

Scrambling to her feet she looked up at him, suddenly trusting, and she felt her heart swell with relief. She knew he was a good man and she laughed, a child-chuckle that echoed round the old stone walls.

He turned towards the altar and gathered her flowers.

"Shall we put them in water?"

She twirled around and then gasped. She pivoted more slowly on her toes, her eyes widening. Sun streamed through the sparkling stained-glass windows, showering rainbows in the dust-mote air. The pews gleamed, newly polished and, as she glanced at her feet balanced on tip-toes, she saw the scrub-washed flagstones.

Wonderingly, she turned and watched as the man lifted the daffodils and placed them in two silver vases, fluted edges splayed wide, either side the cross which rested on a finely stitched golden lace cloth draping the altar and fluttering in the breeze of his movement.

He stood back surveying his arrangements, tweaking a flower head and then looked at her, smiling.

"There, doesn't that look better?"

She nodded, dumbfounded. Then a whisper emerged: "But..?"

"Come, little one." He held out his hand. "Come outside."

She took his hand and walked out through the door. She let out a deep breath. The dell looked normal. Celandines ran riot in the young grass, firs whispered sombrely in the breeze and, below, the river tumbled tranquilly over boulders.

They walked to the river's edge, to a small plateau, across which stretched the trunk of a fallen tree. A tree she had sat on many times and watched the scurrying water and tiny fishes swirling in the eddy as she sorted her jumbled thoughts and tried to understand...

They sat, not touching, but she felt the warmth of his presence, felt his strength in his silence and felt a great door open in her heart.

He waited. She watched a twig float, twirl and rush away and the quiet voice in her head said: "Talk..."

She smiled. The river always brought her peace.

"Gramps said I should talk to...come here..." she tried to explain to the stranger at her side.

"And it was your grandfather you brought the daffodils for?"

She nodded. "He used to carry me on his shoulders," her eyes became dreamy, "high above the briars. Sometimes," she chuckled, "he'd forget how tall I made him and a branch would hit me!" She held her hand to her head. "And I'd nearly fall off. He'd laugh and duck and we'd skim the leaves and when we got here we'd sit on this tree and he'd tell me stories about the spirits."

"The spirits?"

"Of course, the spirits; they live in the trees and grass and flowers," her voice continued in quiet explanation. "And we'd talk to the spirits and thank them for their beauty and he said whenever..." Her voice wobbled.

"Whenever?"

She coughed and kicked her toes. "Whenever I felt sad I was to come and talk to the spirits."

"And you're sad now?"

She nodded as tears welled and trickled gently down her cheeks, dripping onto her arms.

"Because of Gramps?"

"He's gone." Her voice choked. "To live in Heaven, Mummy says."

"Ah, but have you thought that maybe he is here, in the breeze among the flowers he loved and that is why he told you to come back?"

"Gramps, here?" She sounded doubtful as she looked around. She thought for a moment. "Gramps came here as a child, he told me so. And he came to the chapel on Sundays. It was..."

She glanced back at the shadowed walls darkened by trees.

"As you saw it, just now." His voice was gentle and she shifted uncomfortably on the tree trunk.

"Uh huh," she muttered.

There was silence while she contemplated the chapel. "Gramps loved daffodils." She broke the silence. "The first spirits, he called them, the first sign of spring when all the spirits wake up after the winter."

She wiped her tears away, aware that the stranger was watching her. "Mummy cries too," she muttered defensively.

"I'm sure she does. It's all right to cry when you're sad."

"It is?"

He smiled and nodded. "It washes the sadness away."

"Hmm." She thought about his words. "It takes an awful lot of washing," she said eventually.

"Does mummy talk to the spirits?"

Marissa sighed. "Her leg hurts and she can't walk far."

"Then the spirits must go to her."

She stared into the foaming river. "So, I can talk to Gramps here?"

"Why not?"

"Because he won't reply." Her lower lip drooped.

"His words are in your head. Just listen."

"Mmm." She stared at the stones that pierced the rushing water and then sat up straight, "Okay, I'm here, Gramps."

She waited, her eyes on the stranger as he nodded.

"I miss you, Gramps."

A blackbird burst forth in song and a breeze brushed the hair from her face.

"It will get easier." The stranger stroked her cheek and then stood. He turned and walked slowly away, disappearing into the trees.

Marissa stared after him, a frown on her brow; then, with a sigh and a whispered, "Goodbye, Gramps," she turned and walked up to the chapel.

She stood in the darkened doorway for a moment, her heart beating heavily. Had she really seen...? Taking a deep breath, she crept stealthily forward. She stopped, staring at her feet. A broken twig had caught her shoe, leaves whispered away in the draught, dust rising in their wake, disturbed on the grimy slabs.

Slowly she walked towards the altar, her hand trailing the decaying pews, wincing as a sliver of wood snagged her finger.

The cross leaned on the bare altar but...She caught her breath and tiptoed forward. Dulled black vases were full of daffodils, the bright yellow of their petals lifting to catch the sunbeams that filtered through the hole in the window. Holding her breath, she reached upwards and slipped her fingertips over the scalloped edge. She drew back and stared at her fingers. They were wet.

Chuckling gleefully she ran out. The old door, sagging on its hinges, creaked as she passed. Celandines brushed yellow on her ankles as she skipped up the path.

Panting, she reached the top and entered the spinney. She leaned to snap the daffodil stalks, her arm circling to hold the yellow flowers, the sap dripping from the broken stems to stain her skirt.

She ran across the field and into the valley that hid the nestling cottage where her mother would be waiting.

[*I chose this particular story,* Whisper in the Wind, *because it reflects Katy's enjoyment of gentle fantasy and her love of family.*]

SIR HUMPHREY APPLEBY MEETS WILLIAM SHAKESPEARE

Brian Lockett

A street scene

APPLEBY

Good Lord! It's the Bard himself! Good morrow, Master Will.

SHAKESPEARE

Say again.

APPLEBY

I said Good morrow, Master Will.

SHAKESPEARE

Why are you talking in that funny way?

APPLEBY

Well, I assumed you would expect me to address you in the style of the sixteenth century.

SHAKESPEARE

What makes you think we talked like that?

APPLEBY

Well, everybody knows. The plays and so on.

SHAKESPEARE

What plays?

APPLEBY

Your plays, of course. *Measure for Measure*, *Henry V*, *Romeo and Juliet*...the Shakespeare plays, of course.

SHAKESPEARE

Oh, those plays. And you say they were written in a special, weird kind of language? I'm surprised anybody understood them if they were.

APPLEBY

But this is your language. The language of Shakespeare!

SHAKESPEARE

Well, not really.

APPLEBY

What do you mean not really?

SHAKESPEARE

First of all, I didn't write them and secondly, they weren't written in that funny language. Or at least originally.

APPLEBY

I think you'd better explain.

SHAKESPEARE

Sure. A group of us hacks used to meet in a tavern and over a jar or two we'd kick around a few ideas...

APPLEBY

Just a minute. Which 'hacks' would these be?

SHAKESPEARE

Well, apart from myself, there was Kit Marlowe, Frank Bacon, a titled guy whose name I forget and two or three others. Never the same people at each meeting. Anyway, it was great fun and, well, we got a guy to write everything down and get it published.

APPLEBY

But the language! The incomparable language of Shakespeare!

To be, or not to be,—that is the question—
Whether 'tis nobler in the mind to suffer
The slings and arrows of outrageous fortune,
Or to take arms against a sea of troubles,
And by opposing end them ?

SHAKESPEARE

Don't tell me! *Titus Andronicus*?

APPLEBY

No. *Hamlet*. Surely you remember?

SHAKESPEARE

I certainly remember *Hamlet*. Isn't that the one where this foreign guy has a thing about his mother who's married his uncle whose brother died from an ear infection? Boy, did we have trouble with that one. Took us four or five meetings to agree the storyline. I was more comfortable with some of the shorter stuff—sonnets, I think we called them. Do you remember *You remind me of when it was hot*?

APPLEBY

Do you mean *Shall I compare thee to a summer's day?*

SHAKESPEARE

That's it! And what about *Don't let me get in the way if you really want to make it together?*

APPLEBY

I suppose you are referring to *Let me not to the marriage of true minds admit impediment?*

SHAKESPEARE

Bang on. Say, you're really good at this. But enough of me. What do you do?

APPLEBY

Me? I am Secretary to the Cabinet.

SHAKESPEARE

What's that?

APPLEBY

Well, I am the most senior civil servant in the country. I attend meetings of the Cabinet, which is a group of the most important Ministers of the Crown, who, under the chairmanship of the Prime Minister, formulate government policy, present it to the nation and monitor its implementation.

SHAKESPEARE

Doesn't sound a load of laughs to me. But what do you actually do?

APPLEBY

As I've said, I am Secretary to the Cabinet.

SHAKESPEARE

Let me try again. Do you make decisions on how the country is run?

APPLEBY (horrified)

No. That is for Ministers.

SHAKESPEARE

Do you give them money so that they can do what they want to do?

APPLEBY

No. That is for the Chancellor of the Exchequer.

SHAKESPEARE

Do you sack them if they make a mess of things?

APPLEBY

No. That is for the Prime Minister.

SHAKESPEARE

Do you write anything?

APPLEBY

Of course, all the time. I am responsible for writing the minutes.

SHAKESPEARE

Ah! So you're a scribe. You just write down what they say.

APPLEBY

Good Lord, no! Some of them can hardly string two sentences together, let alone produce a coherent and convincing exposition of what passes for ideas. My job is to bring order, balance and structure to what are often inane ramblings in an attempt to present to the nation government policies which will enhance the reputation of Ministers, contribute to the prosperity of the country and ensure, as far as possible, that Her Majesty's subjects are treated fairly, humanely and consistently in their relations with those responsible for the administration of those policies.

SHAKESPEARE

Sounds great. You certainly have a way with words. So it looks as though nothing has changed.

APPLEBY

What do you mean?

SHAKESPEARE

Well, we didn't call ourselves a Cabinet, but we were certainly the sort of people you describe as Ministers—what was that you said about 'inane ramblings'? That was certainly us.

APPLEBY

I'd rather you didn't quote me on that. Perhaps I've said more than I should. In any event, you have taken those words out of context.

SHAKESPEARE

All I'm saying is that you work for a group of people who aren't up to doing what you do. And we ideas men (if you like) had a guy who did just the same for us. I can't remember his name and I don't suppose anyone will remember yours. That's about it, isn't it?

APPLEBY

I suppose it is.

SHAKESPEARE

Anyway, I don't suppose it matters too much, does it? It's just a question of words, isn't it?

APPLEBY (thoughtfully)

Words. Yes. *The rest is silence.*

SHAKESPEARE

Now that I do remember! Great line, don't you think? Nice meeting you. Mind how you go.

[*My piece was created as an exercise in putting two well known characters together and seeing what happens.*]

THE POP STAR AND THE BUSINESS MAN
Elizabeth Ducie

Arthur's heart sank as the train pulled into Reading station. The platform was heaving with festival goers; it was Tuesday, the day after Bank Holiday Monday and even someone who'd been on another planet for the past two weeks and didn't know anything about the annual music festival would have been able to work out that something had been going on. It wasn't usual to see this busy commuter station packed with—well, 'hippies' wasn't a word one heard very often, but it was the only one Arthur could bring to mind. Groups of young people were leaning against pillars, sprawling across seats—not that there were many of those in Reading these days—or sitting on the floor. Some were chatting animatedly, and one large group near the platform for the Gatwick Express were singing along to a guitar, but most were dozing where they stood, or staring into space. It looked like most of them hadn't slept for several days—and even without being close enough to check, Arthur knew they wouldn't have been too fussed about hygiene at the festival grounds either.

The train sat at platform 4 for several minutes, while the announcer told 'customers' there was a problem with a signal further down the line and they were held up by another train just ahead of them. He apologised for 'any inconvenience caused' but it didn't sound as though he meant it; it was more a case of 'I've got to sit here on this train and put up with it, so everyone else has to as well.'

One or two of the festival goers got on the train; Arthur left his briefcase and mackintosh on the seat next to him and buried his nose in his newspaper. A couple of people slowed as they approached him and looked pointedly at him—he could see their reflection in the window—but he ignored them and they moved on to other parts of the train, leaving him with his precious double seat to himself. He had been doing this journey for years now and no-one's stares had any effect on him; it was a point of honour to maintain the empty seat next to him for as many days as possible. Today would make it twenty-five—nearly a month—and a personal record for him. He smiled to himself and made a note in his virtual notebook to brag to Billy Jones when they got to work the next day.

Just then three things happened at once: the guard blew the whistle, the train gave a lurch as the brakes were released prior to starting off—and the carriage door was yanked open. A tall balding man in jeans and a polo-necked jumper flung himself onto the train and slammed the door shut, just as the train began to move. He walked straight over to Arthur's seat, picked up the briefcase and mackintosh and dropped them on the table with a "you don't mind do you, mate?" and subsided into the seat with a massive sigh.

Arthur stared at him in consternation: it wasn't the fact that this man had touched his things, although that was sacrilege on a British train; it wasn't the fact that he'd lost his precious empty seat and with it his chance to snatch the record off Billy Jones; it wasn't even the fact that this was obviously someone from the festival and was therefore not the freshest-smelling passenger with whom to spend a journey. No, it was the fact that Arthur knew this man; he had spent his teenage years with his picture pinned up on his wall; he had bought all his records and had once saved up his pocket money for three months in order to buy a ticket to a concert in Plymouth. This was Jet Stevens, lead singer of the Granite Elephants, hero of many a 1960s teenager; and therefore always 21 in their eyes. He couldn't be an ageing festival goer. It wasn't right—and it was too much of a reminder to Arthur that he was no longer a teenager either.

"God, that was terrible," the words ricocheted around the compartment. Arthur looked up from his newspaper—he'd been staring at it unseeingly, trying to decide whether to speak to this living legend or to ignore him. His inclination was leaning towards the latter, but Jet had taken the decision out of his hands.

"What, the station? Yes, Reading's always busy at this time of day, but it's especially bad today—the festival you know." Arthur groaned inwardly; how could he try to tell Jet Stevens about a music festival?

"No, not the station, man; I could handle the station. I'm talking about the festival."

"Oh, right," Arthur murmured.

"It's all my manager's fault," Jet continued. Arthur looked around wildly. Everyone else was studiously avoiding his eyes, but he was fairly sure they were all listening intently. "I told him it was a mistake booking me in to Reading. But would he listen? Would he ever?" Arthur cleared his throat and shook his newspaper irritably. "I told him they wouldn't have heard of me—and I was right."

"But everyone's heard of you, haven't they?" The words were out of Arthur's mouth before he could stop them. "You're Jet Stevens." Jet swivelled in his seat and stared at Arthur open-mouthed.

"Fancy a suit like you knowing who I am."

"Are you kidding? I've got every one of your albums—even that odd one you did during your punk phase—and I've seen you play live many times over the years." He glanced down at his suit and briefcase and smiled ruefully, "I didn't always dress like this, you know."

"Man, I could have done with you at the festival," said Jet, "and a few of your friends as well. They put me on during the day—late morning, in fact. Half the kids were still in bed and those that were up and about seemed more interested in finding some breakfast than listening to my music. Someone told me they were 'like really, really tired'!"

"Not like the Isle of Wight '73 then?"

"You were there?" Arthur nodded and Jet grinned as he went on. "Wow, yeah, that was some gig. I reckon there was so much dope being smoked there, the seagulls must have been stoned for a week after we'd left."

"Not to mention the old girls from the sea-front."

"Right! The ones that tutted every time we walked past. I don't think they appreciated our music at all, did they?"

"And they didn't like you here, then?"

"Well, if I'm honest, the reception wasn't too bad once I'd got started. They clapped politely when I came on, but were cheering by the time I finished. I even heard one or two brave souls singing along with the chorus of *Brighton Belle*."

"Oh, I've done that once or twice myself. *Brighton Belle, you can go to hell.*"

"*I'm off to see the world!*" Jet joined in. Arthur looked around, a bit embarrassed at being caught singing on the 5:37 from Paddington to Exeter St David, but noticed that the few people who did meet his eye (it was that sort of train) were actually grinning and one woman at the other end of the compartment was also singing along. Arthur suddenly didn't feel like a bank manager for the Kensington branch of a high street bank; he was right back to his student days.

"I saw you perform that live in Regent's Park," he said. Jet looked confused, but Arthur nodded confirmation. "I was at Bedford College, on the Outer Circle. We used to have live bands on stage every Sunday. I saw Elkie Brooks when she was singing with Vinegar Joe; my namesake Arthur Brown with his Crazy World; I even saw Hawkwind one night—no, I tell a lie; that was at one of the University College gigs; I bopped to Tiger Feet when Mud came to play at our Christmas Party; and I was there when you guys did your surprise appearance at the charity gig. I hadn't wanted to go; I was working for an exam the following week but my flatmates convinced me to pop out for a quick pint—and I was so glad I did."

"God yes, I'd forgotten that; someone had to drop out and they asked us at the last minute. I seem to remember we raised a lot of money that evening."

"And then, when you did the Brighton Belle tour, I skipped lectures to queue for tickets. They went on sale in the Virgin Store on Oxford Street at four o'clock in the afternoon and we'd been there since six in the morning. Got told off by a policeman for sitting on the pavement; apparently we were making the place look untidy! But it was worth it—and we got ace seats."

Jet stood up and gave himself a shake. "I need some coffee, man; can I get you some?" As he headed off towards the buffet car, he seemed unaware of the eyes following him and the smiles lighting up the carriage. 'Looks like we've got a whole bunch of ageing hippies on here,' thought Arthur.

When Jet came back with two sealed cups of coffee and a brown paper bag full of nibbles, he seemed to be a bit more relaxed. Arthur told him he hadn't realised the Granite Elephants were still performing live.

"We're not; we've not been on stage all together since the big bust-up in 1983, although three of us got together and did a bit of a tribute when Antony died. Joey plays with another band now, and Vinnie's pretty much retired—his health's not good, I'm afraid." He paused and they paid silent tribute to missing band members. "It's just me that wanted to get back on the road, really. But I'm not sure this new manager of mine is going to work out."

"Not getting you enough work?"

"No, quite the opposite. It was him that got me the Reading gig—but it's not what I want any more. I don't want to play big stadia or packed festival grounds. I certainly don't want to go on tour—and I'm not interested in going down the celebrity reality show route."

"So we're not going to see you on *Strictly* any time soon then?" Arthur grinned.

"God forbid! No, I just want to perform to small crowds of fans who like my music—like we did in the early days." Jet sighed and picked up his coffee. "But I guess it's not possible to turn back the clock like that, is it?"

"Well, you could come and play at Barnfest for starters," Arthur said.

"Never heard of it! What is it; some sort of farming festival?"

"Not quite. I live in a little town on the edge of Dartmoor called Barnfield. We have a ten-day festival in May each year; concerts, quizzes, writing competitions for the kids, that sort of thing. But we try to have one live concert during the week. It would be great if you would agree to come and top the bill for us. But I guess that might be too small for you. Forget I mentioned it."

But Jet assured Arthur he thought it was a great idea and once he'd run it past his manager, he'd get back to him. Before Jet alighted from the train at Tiverton Parkway, he took a copy of Arthur's card—he always carried a bunch of Barnfest cards as well as his bank ones, just in case. As the train pulled out of the station, Jet was standing waving goodbye.

Arthur assumed that was the last he would hear from the ageing pop star, but three days later when he got home, his wife was standing on the doorstep waiting for him, her eyes sparkling and a huge grin on her face.

"You'll never guess who I've been chatting to this afternoon," she said as she kissed his cheek and took his briefcase out of his grasp.

And nine months later, Jet Stevens of the Granite Elephants headlined at the Barnfest opening night concert. Arthur and his wife were sitting in the front row, with a crowd of their friends, all of a similar age. There was a lot of grey hair in the room, both on stage and in the audience. But there were no suits and very few ties in evidence. And when they all joined in the chorus of *Brighton Belle* at the end of the first set, you could hear them half way across Devon.

[*Katy loved all types of music and we often reminisced about the songs we danced to when growing up. She was an avid fan of BBC Radio 2's quiz* Pop Master. *I think she would enjoy the nostalgia in my story.*]

AT THE ELEVENTH HOUR

Val Williamson

Bazzer was late. His stomach was telling him it was way past dinner time, and his mouth craved lubrication.

Having only the haziest recollection of Geordie's instructions, Bazzer had already completed an unplanned tour of the East coast town. It looked bleak and inhospitable, in itself not worth the long trip even in summer. Souvenir shops were boarded up and amusement arcades unlit, everything shuttered against bitter November winds blustering direct from Scandinavia.

"But you *must* remember! You said Thursday the eleventh, at four o'clock."

Bazzer swung himself aggressively off the seat, squaring his shoulders as he confronted Geordie. It had been a long hard ride and he was in no mood for arguments. The seaside wasn't Bazzer's scene at the best of times, not even for a Bank Holiday get-together, and now it seemed obvious that this trip had been a mistake in more ways than one.

"No I didn't!" Geordie insisted, his determined chin jutting his thick beard forward, "I said *Friday*, Friday the twelfth. Thursdays are dangerous—and it's hours past four, now."

Bazzer couldn't believe he could have come on the wrong day. And what did Geordie mean by "Thursdays are dangerous"?

"Well I've got to be back by tomorrow night, so it's now or never."

"We'll just have to make the best of it, then," Geordie conceded.

Bazzer's custom project wasn't a distance bike, not a traveller. Journeying over fifty miles in winter was not what he'd had in mind when he built it. He'd never have contemplated riding it all this way if Geordie hadn't promised to introduce him to the best motorbike artist in the world.

"This bloke, Tor, he not only paints themes to order, he can even help you dream up exactly the right theme for you," Geordie had promised, during that first drunken encounter. "But he's busy with the fair in summer. You'll have to come in a couple of months' time, when the season's over."

Being not only totally pissed, but also thoroughly pissed off at the time, Bazzer had agreed the arrangements. In the drunken haze of that first meeting with Geordie, Bazzer had been obsessed with the fact that, at the rally earlier that day, his project had once again failed to win any of the prizes he felt it deserved. Not that Bazzer had embarked on the project with prize winning in mind, but his mate Vinny had harboured ambitions, and Bazzer had really wanted to win something for him. The fault, as Geordie had been quick to point out, lay not in the unique design of the machine, but in the amateurish and unimaginative paint job.

Imagination was no more Bazzer's strong point than listening attentively. He'd been building and rebuilding this bike for eleven years, but he couldn't have said what its theme was, only whether he liked the finished effect or not. Vinny had been full of ideas for themes, seeming to come up with a new vision every week, but he never got round to putting anything down on paper.

With Vinny's enthusiasm in mind, and the dreary winter months already seeming to drag, Bazzer had made a snap decision to seek out the artist who'd done an award-winning job on Geordie's project. That was a unique design, too, painted mainly in silver and black. "I call it *Neptune's Messenger*," Geordie explained.

"*Silver Fish* would be more like it," Bazzer had argued. A close-up of Neptune, seaweed crown and all, leered out from the fat-bob, but the overall appearance was of a giant fish or dolphin, right down to the split tail points curving either side the rear wheel.

An investigation of the depths of Bazzer's pockets had turned up the scrap of paper with Geordie's address on it. But, on the journey here, it wasn't only the weather which had induced the depression that had descended. It had suddenly dawned on Bazzer that once Geordie had introduced him to this bloke, Tor, and they'd agreed on the decoration, that would be it. Eleven years of his life would be over.

They rode the Prom alongside a bottomless pit that spat salt water in their faces. Far in the blackness beyond the reach of the street lighting, surf crashed destructively on the beach. The silver fish led the way, taking the brunt, but the wind-whipped sea spray spattering Bazzer's jacket and visor made him shudder and wish for the comforts of his own home city. However, his memories of the bright lights and raucous sounds of many a fairground kept him glued to Geordie's tail as they set off to seek out Tor.

The fairground was disappointingly dark and broodily silent as they rode the perimeter fence, until they passed between high shabby sagging doors. Not far inside a stooped, gnomish figure waited by a ride shrouded in canvas, the scenario illuminated only by the beams from their headlamps.

"So, it's a naming of themes, is it?"

The wizened and decidedly vertically disadvantaged old fellow didn't even try to inspect Bazzer's bike. He looked hard at Bazzer, though. Straight into Bazzer's eyes, with Bazzer just sitting there, staring straight back. If he hadn't been so mesmerised Bazzer might have wondered why the old fellow's eyes were so startlingly blue, and how he could have noticed the fact without benefit of proper illumination.

"We'd better get on with it, then!"

This was the signal for them to retire into a nearby hut where, by some miracle, Tor had a crate of Bazzer's favourite bevy. They settled down to some serious supping, but the melancholic realisation that the project was over didn't leave Bazzer. Several pints, and a parcel of fish and chips later, he found himself giving details of how he'd constructed the bike.

He threw it all in—how he had come across the improbable double-width engine; who he had found to customize a frame for it. How, at one time, he'd fitted an extended shovel-head front, and why he'd had to alter that when he had welded on what now looked like the back half of a Mini car.

"It's a trike now," Bazzer said, "I changed it so I could take my mate Vinny to biker rallies."

Vinny had driven his machine to the limits and paid the price. He never felt the throb of an engine under him again, but once a biker always a biker. He had lived for Bazzer's project after that, even suggested how to incorporate parts of his wreck into it, so that it became his project, too.

Mind you, Vinny had laughed long and hard each winter when Bazzer ritually reduced the project to a rubble of spare parts, and began struggling to incorporate ill thought out changes into the rebuild. Most often it was Vinny who came up with ingenious solutions to Bazzer's self inflicted problems. Vinny had been full of imagination and brimming with suggestions for the final paint job too, but time ran out for him.

"As usual," Bazzer continued, "I hadn't listened carefully and, what with the grief, I've no clear memory of what he wanted."

"Right," said Geordie, getting to his feet, "it's eleven o'clock."

"Time for the naming," Tor said. "Put your helmet on, Bazzer, you'll need it." He led the way out to pull back the canvas from the ride.

Bazzer didn't know what he'd expected. The Waltzers or a Caterpillar ride, perhaps, or even a Wall of Death, but not this.

"A carousel!"

He swore angrily at the sight of the painted ponies, at the gold candy-twist poles which gleamed when the lights winked on, at the stately barrel-organ tune which sprang from behind twin large-eyed statues of musicians at the hub. It wasn't even a modern contraption, with metal or fibreglass horses. These ponies were individually carved, end-of-season flaking paint revealing bare wood underneath.

"Thursdays are more powerful, you know that?' Tor's seriousness silenced Bazzer's protests as he allowed his leather-clad helmeted self to be led up the steps. Bazzer climbed on the nearest painted horse that sported a gold twisted pole like a unicorn's horn, silently giving thanks that there were so few people to observe this act of stupidity, and thankful that Tor and Geordie were mounting too. The carousel began to turn.

No doubt booze, and tiredness, contributed. Certainly they were bound to exaggerate the effect of the travelling round and round and of the pony dipping up and down, up and down to the ceaseless reverberation of the barrel-organ waltz. But that didn't begin to explain what happened next.

Soon Bazzer's eyes could no longer focus, not even on the pony in front, and the music had become so much background noise. Speed was the reason, the sort of speed he had never even dreamed of. The sort of speed that leaves the stomach travelling separately, at a distant point behind its owner. The sort of speed that completely scrambles the brain.

Geordie and Tor were still with him, Bazzer registered, and the musicians still stared, but transformed into Viking warriors. Bazzer seemed to fly off with them into the unknown, traversing a flaming sea in a long narrow boat with a bulging sail that cracked and popped like a motor with faulty timing. Just as his recently returned stomach threatened to rebel against the endless rising and dipping, the boat dematerialised and left him standing, gaping, between the fat candy-twist pillars of a huge doorway.

The hall was lined with spears standing on end against a wall of light and supporting a ceiling of overlapped shields. Helmets were stacked everywhere; Viking helmets, made of leather banded with metal, but there were other types too, of warriors from ages past, and from wars fought not so long ago. And bikers' helmets of every shape and kind. And bikers' voices, and engines revving and familiar faces, though long unseen, beneath shining Viking helmets—and Vinny. Not the Vinny who had never really recovered from the accident, but a great strapping healthy Vinny in full Viking gear. Tor seemed to have expanded, too, his face no longer wizened, his eyes brighter and bluer than ever. He was the mightiest one, the sword-bearer, the one in charge of Valhalla, which Bazzer was sure was where they were.

A great cheer went up when Tor was revealed in all his glory, and then the horn of plenty started its rounds. Bazzer couldn't work out what was in it, but it blended well with what he had supped already. During the mock battle with spears and shields Geordie had to restrain him. "Steady, mate, we're not immortal, like this lot!"

So Bazzer took it steady after that, much to Vinny's amusement, and then in came the cattle. Vinny made it look easy, riding the back of a bucking steer better than he'd ever handled his bike, but he was thrown after a few minutes. Nobody managed to make a beast look tameable until Tor took his turn. He easily controlled his mount, looking as good as any Grand National jockey.

"Mount up!" he called, his eyes lighting brilliantly on Bazzer.

Bazzer looked round, but there was nobody behind him. "Who, me?" he queried incredulously, wondering how he could leap high enough in the air to even come close to riding the beast nearest to him.

"Just shut your eyes and go for it," Geordie advised, eyeing a similar animal.

Bazzer took one more swig from the drinking horn that had miraculously appeared in his hand, closed his eyes, and launched himself. He hadn't expected to last two seconds on the hard-ridged but glossily hairy back, but the creature settled immediately, then bore Bazzer forward, undulating in a gentle up-and-down motion. Nevertheless, Bazzer kept his eyes closed until the stately barrel-organ sound impinged on his consciousness. He shook his head disbelievingly as the shabby old carousel slid gently to a halt and his wooden mount tilted to gently tip him off.

"So, the theme is named," Tor, reduced to the wizened original, stated. "Leave the machine with me overnight. You can collect it tomorrow, at noon."

"Tomorrow? But won't it take days? For the paint to dry—that'll take days, even weeks—won't it?"

"Give him a lift on your machine, Geordie. Tomorrow, at noon," Tor concluded, firmly.

And on Friday, at noon, Bazzer took possession of his transformed machine.

When he got home to the city, Bazzer parked the trike near the jar on the ledge at the crematorium that was all that remained of Vinny.

"I love it," Bazzer said, "it couldn't be better. That Tor is some artist. I should have known, Vinny, he pronounces his name 'Tor' but he spells it with an 'h' after the 'T'. Lucky for you I went on Thursday—*Thor's* day. You always fancied yourself as Vinny the Viking, didn't you? I remembered in the end, you see."

Painted flames licked round the battle chariot that the trike had become, and the towering warrior depicted on the petrol tank looked like Vinny, but now Bazzer knew that the project wasn't finished at all. At the eleventh minute of the eleventh hour of the eleventh day of the eleventh month he had seen Tor's engraved metal armlets, and Vinny's, and had realised that there were a few vital elements missing.

"I wonder who I can find to engrave the engine casings?" Bazzer said, "and make handlebars shaped like bull's horns, or headlamp casings like Viking helmets?"

As Bazzer gunned life into the engine he heard somebody laughing.

It was the sort of rumbling belly laugh guaranteed to out-thunder the most powerful motor.

The sort of laugh that might echo all the way from Valhalla.

[*My fiction ideas often spring from my experiences in the many and varied jobs I have done and people I have met in my journey through life. This story draws on my experiences over the several years I worked as a part-time social worker in a large bikers' club at the end of the 1960s. I wrote it twenty five years ago, in the year I met Katy at her, and my, very first Swanwick. Accepted for publication by a biker magazine, but never published, it is a fantasy story about mixed emotions: the grief of loss and the joy of remembrance.*]

ZOE'S BIRTHDAY TREAT

Julia Pattison

"One more sleep till my birthday!" squealed Zoe with excitement as she jumped into her cosy bed.

"Not long now," agreed her Mum with a smile, "which story are you going to choose tonight then?"

"The Lion Who Lost His Roar!" said Zoe without a moment's hesitation. "My favourite!"

Zoe loved lions. She had a whole collection of cuddly lion toys, and her bedroom was decorated with various pictures and posters of her favourite animal.

So, for a special birthday treat, Zoe's Mum and Dad were taking her to see the Chinese State Circus, featuring a spectacular Lion Dance. No wonder Zoe was excited!

At last, after all the anticipation, Zoe was sitting in her ringside seat, eating candy floss, eagerly waiting for the performance to start.

Suddenly the spotlights snapped on, and a troupe of acrobats wearing sparkly sequined costumes burst into the circus ring.

"Ladies and Gentlemen, Boys and Girls," a cheerful voice boomed over the loudspeakers, "welcome to the Chinese State Circus!"

After that, everything happened in a whirl for Zoe. The acrobats bounded and leapt around the circus ring, performing daring tricks with graceful ease; Zoe watched, spellbound.

All too soon it was the interval and, as part of the birthday treat, her Dad took her to the souvenir stall to choose a present to remind her of her visit. Zoe was so busy looking at all the lovely items on sale that she didn't notice her Mum sneaking off to have a word with one of the circus crew.

Finally, Zoe chose a framed photograph of the Chinese Lion due to be performing that night.

As she waited for the show to begin again, she studied every detail of her precious souvenir. The Lion was brightly coloured with a huge body and head—the head particularly fascinated her with its bulging spiral eyes, and large red mouth complete with giant white teeth. Zoe was both nervous, and excited, at the thought of seeing this Lion so close to her soon.

A gong sounded, indicating that the second half was about to begin. How Zoe laughed as the Chinese Clowns fooled around while the Rope Performers prepared themselves for their breath-taking act.

She sat open-mouthed as a young Chinese girl in a sparkly red costume seemed to tie herself in knots, smiling sweetly as the audience applauded.

Then...the moment she had been waiting for—the Chinese Lion Dance! One of the acrobats led the enormous Lion into the circus ring. Zoe felt her foot tapping as the percussion rhythm got faster and faster. The Lion bounded this way and that, leaping high into the air.

Without warning though, it suddenly leapt towards Zoe and stopped just centimetres away from her nose; Zoe shut her eyes and held tightly onto her Mum's hand, not daring to move.

When she opened them again, she laughed in joy and relief as the enormous red mouth opened, revealing a Chinese acrobat inside, who gave Zoe a friendly wink.

A deep voice came over the loudspeakers: "The Chinese Lion wishes Zoe a very Happy Birthday!"

"How did they know it was my birthday?" gasped Zoe in surprise.

"Aha!" said her Mum with a twinkle in her eye. Leaping back into the circus ring, the Chinese Lion continued to entertain everyone with its antics.

At the end of the performance the crowd clapped and cheered loudly as several very hot acrobats emerged from underneath the Lion costume, beaming broadly.

Zoe thought she would burst with pride when they all winked and waved at her before leaving the circus ring.

This was the best birthday she'd ever had.

[*I met Katy in 2004 and we soon discovered we had much in common; a love of music, myths and dance. We both loved letting out the inner child and never reached the age of not believing! This children's short story is dedicated to Zoe, Katy Clarke's beloved granddaughter.*]

A SURPRISE IN THE JUNGLE

Pat Belford

The animals were upset. After a hot day in the jungle they had come down to the clearing to drink in the river pool and found the water thick with mud.

"Those hippos have been swimming in our pool again," Lion growled.

"Something will have to be done," Elephant said. "It's the third time this week!"

"I'm SO thirsty!" Little Monkey moaned.

"You must not drink that muddy water," Mother Monkey told him.

The animals turned away, sadly. They filed up a jungle path to a tiny waterfall and took turns to drink, but it wasn't as good as the river pool.

Little Monkey took a few sips of water then scampered up into a tree and gazed around as the sky became darker. Suddenly he sat up. He could see a pale shape which he didn't recognise in the distance.

"There's something over there in the jungle—a strange white creature!" he whispered, scrambling out of the tree.

"What sort of creature?" asked Lion.

"It's white and it's moving. Look!"

The animals stopped drinking and stared. Even though it was dark they all saw the white shape amongst the shadowy trees.

"There are no white animals living in our jungle," Elephant said. "What can it be?"

"I'm going to investigate," Lion said and he marched bravely down the path. The others followed, not feeling brave at all. The white thing was still flitting through the bushes.

"It's coming nearer!" Little Monkey shrieked and climbed onto his mother's back.

"It's heading for the river!"

As the animals reached the muddy river pool, a beautiful white creature stepped into the clearing. It looked like a small horse but the moonlight gleamed on a pointed horn that grew in the middle of its forehead.

"What is that?" asked Little Monkey.

"It's a..." Lion began.

"I think it's a..." Elephant said.

"I'm a unicorn," the animal said shyly. "Why are you all staring at me?"

"A unicorn? We've never seen a unicorn before," Lion said.

"I didn`t mean to trouble you," the unicorn said. "I have travelled a long way and I am tired and thirsty. I'm looking for a drink and somewhere to stay."

"Don't drink from this pool," Lion warned. "The hippos have used it for bathing and made it muddy."

The unicorn seemed not to have heard. It stepped forward and dipped its horn in the muddy water. At once, the pool became so clear that the white pebbles on the bottom of the river could be seen shining in the moonlight.

"Look...it's magic!" Little Monkey whispered.

"How did you do that?" Lion asked.

"All unicorns can purify water with their horns," said Unicorn and he took a long drink.

The animals drank, too. The water felt deliciously cool.

"Unicorn, you are welcome to stay in the jungle with us," Lion said.

"Thank you. Can I sleep here by the pool?" Unicorn stepped out of the water.

"Of course. I'll stay here too, to keep guard, then perhaps the hippos will keep to their own part of the river," Lion said.

The unicorn lay down on the grass and yawned.

"Goodnight, sleep well!" Little Monkey called, and he yawned, too.

"Time you were in bed, Little Monkey!" Mother Monkey said and she carried him back into the jungle.

[As a Swanwicker of long standing I, like many others, remember hearing Katy sing at our farewell parties. A few years ago, when we were both tutoring four part courses, we would meet up daily at the end of our respective sessions to compare notes.]

SPREADING MAGIC

Helen Ellwood

Teasel sighed and stamped his silver hoof in frustration. Another boring evening looking after his baby sister stretched ahead, while his parents pranced about in the lake, gathering moonbeams. He longed to be like them, shining silver-white in the moonlight. He watched as they dipped their slender horns into the water, turning their heads this way and that to harvest the magic. His legs still felt far too long for his body and his coat still had the occasional patch of pink left over from childhood. He'd been busy for the last half hour, trying to pull a tuft out from his flank, but no matter how he chewed at it and tugged at it, a few wisps of annoying fluff remained.

He glanced down at his younger sister. She had the short, fat, dumpy legs and bright pink coat of a baby. Her mane and tail were all the colours of the rainbow instead of the pure white they would become. She was dancing on the pebbles at the edge of the lake, dipping her horn into the water, scattering the moon's reflections. She tossed her mane, squeaking with delight as droplets of water turned into rainbows.

"It's not fair," he said. "Why do I always have to look after you while the grown-ups are busy?"

His sister gazed up at him with huge, bright eyes. "Because Mummy says so."

"Yes but..."

"And Daddy says so."

"But you're safe playing on your own, aren't you?" said Teasel.

"Of course I am. I'm nearly two."

Just then, she slipped on a rock and fell into the shallow water with a cry. Teasel rushed forward and helped her up again. He checked her knees for grazes and licked her tears away.

"It's alright, Baby. You're not hurt."

"I'm all wet. And my name isn't Baby."

"But your proper name is such a mouthful. I like the name Baby. It suits you. Once you're grown up like me, I shall use your full magical name, but for now, you're Baby."

His sister planted her tiny pink hooves on the ground, took a deep breath and...

"Don't cry," said Teasel. "Please don't cry. Look, if you can find me a pebble with a hole all the way through it, you'll get a prize."

Baby pranced off, happy again.

The surrounding forest was almost as clear as day, lit with the fine, silver light of the full moon. Faeries flitted through the trees, laughing and casting playful magic without a care. Teasel felt as though he was the only creature in the whole Fey world not having fun. As he yanked petulantly at another tuft of pink fluff on his side, an idea began to form in his mind.

A few moments later, Baby bounced up to him, dropping a perfectly round pebble at his hooves. Through the centre was a perfectly round hole.

"Where's my prize?" she said, looking up at him. Her little, tufted ears pricked forward and her long, thick mane fell to one side, curling in swirls of violet and blue.

"Let's make a portal," he said, "and visit the mortal world."

"Are we allowed?"

"No."

Baby's ears flicked back. "Then we shouldn't. Not if it's dangerous."

"But dangerous can be fun," said Teasel, tossing his mane with impatience. His forelock had grown so long, his eyes were almost hidden. "It's so boring here. Faeries, Pixies, moonlight, blah blah."

"If we go, can I bring a human back as a pet?"

"No. We're just going have a look. That's all."

"Shall I go and tell Mummy?"

"Mummy doesn't need to know. I'll keep you safe, I promise. Remember the rules. We mustn't do any spells, we mustn't leave a trace of anything magical in their world and we mustn't be seen."

Baby nodded.

Feeling elated that something exciting was going to happen at last, Teasel drew a circle in the air with his horn, creating a swirl of coloured lights. Without hesitation, both unicorns ran straight through.

They landed in the grounds of a grand country house. Behind them, the portal took the form of a circular rose arch, shining white in the light of the moon. Baby trampled around in the rose bed, gazing in wonder at the sloping lawns and flowers. She was surprised to see how pleasant it was.

She'd expected monsters.

"Are we going to explore?" she said.

"Just a little," said Teasel, "but I'd better stay near the portal. I'll call if I see a human. You must run to me straight away and don't go too far."

Baby nodded her head, pricking her ears forward to show she was listening, but all she could think about was needing the toilet. It was probably all the candy floss she'd eaten earlier. She knew if she told Teasel, he'd make her go home, right now. Nothing from the immortal world was allowed in the human realm. Not even a single rainbow coloured hair. But she didn't want to go back yet. They'd only just arrived.

She cantered to the centre of the lawn. Glancing back, she saw Teasel pacing around the rose arch, looking up at the lighted windows in the house. Was he scared? What was so terrible about humans anyway? They weren't big or covered in scales like dragons and they weren't clever and filled with magic like Elves.

She hid herself in the middle of a bed of tall flowers, making sure Teasel couldn't see her, and lifted her multicoloured tail. When she'd finished, she gave a little shake of her rump, and jumped back onto the lawn. No-one would notice. Especially if it rained. The sparkles would fade by morning.

Pushing at the door of the big house with her shoulder, she ran inside to find a room with a carpeted floor and many chairs and tables. Another room had glass walls and lots of green plants. And there was one with books in it, some of them filled with fairy tales.

Back outside, she trotted across the lawn. On the other side of the garden was another building with many windows and a locked door. She pressed her nose against it, breathing gently on the numbers that held the magic code. The door opened with a click, allowing her to run along a corridor. She could feel the sleeping humans on either side, each one in their own room. Each one dreaming dreams of fears and problems. She ran up a flight of stairs and back along the upper corridor. It was the same. Many, many human beings and only a few seemed truly happy. She paused. Should she spread a little magic? Just a tiny bit? It was so easy to do; even a baby unicorn could turn sadness to joy and bad fortune to good. It was such a shame it was completely forbidden to do so.

Resisting the temptation to help them, she galloped back out into the garden to find Teasel pacing up and down. His coat shone white and pink in the moonlight. She ran to him.

"We'd better be getting back," he said.

Baby thought he still looked nervous.

"They're all asleep," she panted. "I think they're harmless."

Teasel fixed her with a stern gaze. "It's time to go home."

Back in their own world, Teasel felt relieved. No one had noticed their absence and no harm had been done.

"Can we have another adventure tomorrow night?" said Baby. She was dancing around with glee, splashing in the shallows of the moonlit lake.

"We probably shouldn't do that again," said Teasel. "We were lucky we weren't seen."

"I want to go again."

"We must never go again. It's too risky."

"But you were the one who wanted to go," said Baby.

"I know, but…I got scared."

"There was nothing to be scared of. They were all asleep."

"You don't know that," said Teasel, glancing over to where their parents were still busy gathering moonbeams. "At least we didn't leave any trace."

There was a pause. He looked down at his younger sister. She was pawing her tiny pink hoof along the grass as if searching for daisies. Teasel's heart began to thump.

"We didn't leave any trace, did we?" he repeated.

"Well…"

"What did you do?"

"I may have left a little magic behind. In a flowerbed. I couldn't help it. I had to go. I got all excited and…"

Baby gazed up at Teasel, her eyes shining. Teasel's heart melted. Maybe a tiny bit of magic, hidden away from mortal eyes, was safe enough.

"That's alright," he said. "No harm done. They'll all wake up feeling happy, that's all."

All the resentment he'd felt at having been asked to look after her evaporated as he realised what a brave little unicorn she was. And maybe, just maybe, next month they could spread a little more magic in that garden. Maybe they could break the rules and create one special, magic place in the human world. And maybe, one day, unicorns and humans could even be friends.

[*Katy and I met properly in 2016. She helped me cope when I found I was unable to go to Swanwick at the last minute due to a flare up of my chronic pain condition. She picked me up and held my virtual hand throughout the week. We both put flowers in our hair and sent each other photos of what we were wearing for the virtual fancy dress disco. We met on the virtual lawn for coffee and enjoyed uplifting conversations. She made that week memorable. It was as if I had been to that magical land instead of being alone, at home, in pain. Thank you Katy.*]

BRAMWELL AND THE SPIDER

Julia Pattison

"That's a lovely drawing Bramwell," said Mummy proudly, as she pinned up his latest piece of work on the kitchen wall.

Bramwell loved to draw. He would spend hours drawing all sorts of creatures, such as birds and insects. He wasn't too keen on spiders though; they made him feel a bit nervous, so he avoided drawing them.

"Spiders? Yuk!" he would say with a shudder, if Mummy asked him if he wanted to draw a spider in the garden. "I hate them—horrible creepy crawlies, with long, scary legs."

"Right Bramwell, time to go to school," said Mummy reaching for her winter coat hanging on the peg on the kitchen door.

"Make sure you wrap up warmly, it's bitterly cold today," she warned, as she handed him his coat.

After putting on his coat, Bramwell wrapped his colourful scarf snugly round his neck, then pulled on his woollen hat and gloves. He was glad he'd listened to Mummy's advice as they stepped out of the warmth of the kitchen into the cold, crisp winter air. Brrr!

Every morning on the way to school, Bramwell and Mummy passed a large hedge. In the summer it was green and lush, filled with chattering birds and scurrying insects all seeking shelter from the summer sun. Now the hedge stood stark and still, covered in a blanket of hard winter frost that glistened in the watery winter sunshine.

"Look at this beautiful pattern," said Mummy, pointing to a cobweb sparkling brightly, looking magnificent.

The glinting, delicate web fascinated Bramwell, and he moved closer to the hedge to get a better look.

So absorbed was he by the exquisite patterns of the web, that he forgot to be frightened when the spider, who had been hiding in the hedge, suddenly twirled round and round on his thread, lowering himself at great speed.

"Wow!" said Bramwell, his eyes widening in amazement as the spider swung up and down, then round and round, putting the finishing touches to his web.

"What a clever spider!" he exclaimed. "I wish I could draw something like that."

"Shall I take a photo of it?" suggested Mummy, "then you can draw the spider's web tonight when you get back from school." She took out her mobile phone.

"Yes please," said Bramwell happily.

He drew his picture that night, and Mummy proudly added it to his collection of drawings on the kitchen wall.

Bramwell wasn't frightened of spiders any more.

[*I wrote this short story for children in memory of Katy Clarke who loved nature and also dedicated to my grandson Bramwell who loves nature and stories.*]

A SIGN OF PEACE

Katy Clarke (Catherine McPherson Clarke)

The insignia of my great-grandfather's regiment, the 51st Division of the Seaforth Highlanders, was a cat salient proper and above were the words, *Sans Peur* **(Without Fear).**

Without fear? I don't think any man who fought in the First World War could, in total honesty, say it was without fear.

Perhaps the motto's true meaning in the face of the Great War was that what had to be done should be done in the certain knowledge it was the only way.

Certainly, my great-grandfather, or Papa, as I called him, was the gentlest man I've ever known.

I knew him when the horrors of war were behind him by several decades. My childhood memories of him are as warm as his greenhouse where I forever pottered at this side. He spent hours potting plants and growing tomatoes so delicious I would pluck them straight from the plant and eat them like sweets.

Papa had been a skilled carpenter and cabinet-maker by trade. He had built the greenhouse many years before and often made wooden toys for his great-grandchildren.

When I was 14, Papa died quietly in his sleep. My gran (his daughter) put away one or two mementoes of him. Now, many years later, she has given me one of those keepsakes, and I will treasure it always for what it meant to Papa and for what it represents today.

For Papa, his fighting part in the war came to an abrupt end in 1916. He had fought alongside his kilted regiment as a signalman for two years. Long days and nights were spent standing knee-deep in

the miserable trenches of France.

It must have seemed like a miracle when one day as he was coming back down the line after fighting at the front, he heard a familiar voice call his name. It was his own brother on his way to the front with his regiment. They embraced where they stood, neither knowing if they would see each other again.

Finally, Papa was hospitalized. As he slowly recovered as much as he ever would, he watched men come and go—physically and emotionally violated. Some died, while others were sent back to fight at the front.

Papa's nerves had been shredded with shell-shock and his lungs and stomach severely affected by poisonous gas. He was sent to Calais where he took charge of German prisoners of war. For them, too, the killing had ended. Like our men, they faced lengthy separation from their families.

Perhaps Papa had been chosen because of his quiet understanding. Some of the prisoners were also shell-shocked. So Papa took them to a timber-yard and taught them simple woodwork. Today, it would be called occupational therapy.

Shattered nerves were soothed as they concentrated on carving and handling wood. They used only the simplest makeshift tools. A rapport between the men and Papa meant they began to call him 'Sergeant Jock'. The carpentry lessons produced imaginative results—beautifully crafted dolls and picture frames.

One young prisoner seemed more distant and forlorn than the rest. He looked particularly sad one evening.

Papa asked what was troubling him. The man managed to blurt out enough in broken English to say letters from home were not reaching him and he longed to see his wife again. Then he broke down and cried, "Why we fight, Jock, why we fight?"

Papa put his arm around the prisoner and said he was sure the war would soon be over. He persuaded him to come to 'Sergeant Jock's timber-yard' to make picture frames for his wife—a present for her when he went home.

The prisoner cheered up as he worked wood for the first time and eventually produced a pair of ornately-decorated frames. He had used little more than nails and a pen-knife to do it.

Meanwhile, Papa was being helped through the lasting effects of shell-shock. He was engrossed in teaching his charges out in the open air, away from noise and confined spaces.

When Armistice Day came at last, the war-weary prisoners and their keepers prepared to go their separate ways.

Away from youths screaming for their mothers and the 'him or me' finality of the front, a bond had been formed.

Some of Papa's men came to him as they were released.

"Sergeant Jock, you have been a kind man. We will never forget you," they said, giving him a pair of picture frames.

The last to climb into the truck was the young man Papa had comforted when all had seemed so black without news from home.

"Jock, we should never have been enemies," he said. "Remember me. This is for you." He pressed a small metal box into Papa's hand.

Papa looked at the gift, a matchbox holder, laboriously bent into shape and decorated with his name—Sergeant J. McPherson, 1/5 Seaforth Highlanders, 51st Division.

On the edge of an engraved scroll was Papa's army number, 41564 and the word, Calais. On the front, the cat salient was encircled with the words, *Sans Peur*.

I have that matchbox holder now. Amazingly, when I moved in to my present home, I discovered that my new phone number was identical to Papa's number.

The matchbox holder is cold to the touch, but warms as I hold it in my hand like the warmth and care of fellow human beings. To me it is a legacy of hope in the face of adversity - a tangible memory of Papa's gentleness— the old man I knew who lived the rest of his life *Sans Peur*.

[*This is an article Katy wrote for Woman's Weekly many years ago, about her great grandfather. It captures her love of history, family, humanity, love and peace. It seemed fitting to give Katy the last word in this anthology produced in her memory.*]

ABOUT THE AUTHORS

Pat Belford finds being a children's author very rewarding. Having taught in primary schools in Leeds for many years, she especially enjoys writing fiction for the under–elevens. Her books have been used extensively in UK schools as well as in English speaking countries around the world. She also writes short stories and articles, and has written the librettos for several musical plays for schools. She thinks children love stories which have elements of magic–and unicorns are especially magical!

Elizabeth Ducie had been working in the international pharmaceutical industry for nearly thirty years, when she decided she'd like to take a break from technical writing—text books, articles and training modules—and write about some of her travel experiences instead. She took some courses in Creative Writing and discovered to her surprise that she was happier, and more successful, writing short stories than memoirs or life-writing. In 2012, she gave up the day job, and started writing full-time. So far, she has published three novels, four collections of short stories and a series of ebooks on business skills for writers. Her first novel, *Gorgito's Ice Rink*, was Runner Up in the 2015 Self-Published Book of the Year Awards. Website: elizabethducie.co.uk

Helen Ellwood has had three plays staged by amateur production companies in Derby, has been a member of the script writing team for two BBC funded docudramas and has had two short stories broadcast by BBC Radio Derby; all in the past ten years. She has had a short story published in a science fiction anthology, *After the Fall*, Boo Books. The memoir of her time spent as a castaway on an uninhabited island (*Message in a Bottle*) was long-listed for the Mslexia Memoir Competition 2014. She has just completed a literary horror/romance novel called *The Girl, the Boy and the Breadfruit Tree*, based on her memoir. She is sending this out to agents with her fingers crossed.

Elizabeth Hopkinson has had over 60 short stories published in magazines and anthologies, and has won several prizes, including the James White Award, Jane Austen Short Story (runner-up) and National Gallery Inspiration. Her first novel *Silver Hands* was published by Top Hat Books in 2013 and this year she has published an eBook of previously-published stories, *Tales from the Hidden Grove*. She is currently working on a trilogy inspired by the world of Italian baroque opera. Elizabeth is a regular member of Swanwick Writers' Summer School, and has led a number of workshops there. She lives in Bradford, West Yorkshire, UK, with her husband, daughter and cat, in a tiny house that is being taken over by books and artwork. Website: elizabethhopkinson.uk.

Maggie Kay (Srimati) is Katy's sister. Having grown up in Scotland, Maggie moved to London then Devon, where Katy also settled in recent years. Maggie now lives in Cornwall with husband Pat where she writes and runs Thrivecraft—a life and business coaching retreat and training academy. Formerly an ordained Buddhist, Maggie specialises in meditation, law of attraction and spiritual intelligence. Her new book, *Diving for Pearls: The Wise Woman's Guide to Finding Love*, includes memoirs of her shared spiritual experiences with Katy. Website: maggiekaywisdom.com

Brian Lockett started writing when he retired from full-time employment in the Civil Service in 1989. He now specialises in short stories, which he uploads on YouWriteOn. Email: brian.lockett2@btopenworld.com.

Julia Pattison has been writing children's stories since the birth of her own children, Lara and Matthew, in the eighties. She has enjoyed some publishing success including selling stories to Twinkle magazine and annuals, as well as The Little Storyteller series by Marshall Cavendish. Julia is now inspired to write further children's stories after the birth of her beautiful grandson, Bramwell, in 2016.

Fay Wentworth has had short stories, novellas and articles for children and adults published in magazines, online and in paperback/ebooks. She has pursued her love of creative writing since childhood; her first short story was written at the age of eleven, a tragic tale about a rabbit in a thunderstorm! Website: faywentworth.wordpress.com.

Val Williamson Val Williamson has been writing for prizes and publication since childhood. Her short stories have been published in a variety of magazines and broadcast on BBC radio. Several appear in anthologies, including Richard and Judy's Winning Stories, and a few were recently published as an Amazon ebook, *Night Strike*. Val has also published many short non-fiction articles in online magazines such as Digital Journal, Decoded Science and Decoded Past, or as chapters in academic books.

THE MAGIC OF SWANWICK

Swanwick Writers' Summer School has been captivating audiences for nearly 70 years. Believed to be the longest running residential writers' school in the world, the 'magic of Swanwick' is legendary. For one spell-binding week every August, over 200 published and unpublished writers across all genres gather together to renew old friendships and forge new ones.

Katy Clarke loved Swanwick. She attended regularly for nearly thirty years; was a course tutor on many occasions; sat on the organising committee and served as Chairman during 2007 and 2008 (the Diamond Jubilee year).

Website: swanwickwritersschool.org.uk

Printed in Great Britain
by Amazon